W9-CCR-268

E   KACZMAN, JAMES
KAC   LUCKY MONKEY
      UNLUCKY MONKEY

WITHDRAWN

HUDSON PUBLIC LIBRARY
WOOD SQUARE
HUDSON, MA 01749

For my mom and dad

James Kaczman

LUCKY MONKEY

UNLUCKY MONKEY

A STORY

Houghton Mifflin Company
Boston 2008

HUDSON PUBLIC LIBRARY
WOOD SQUARE
HUDSON, MA 01749

JUN 0 4 2008

Lv cK.
THE MONKEYWORKS

Copyright © 2008 by James Kaczman

All rights reserved. For information about permission to
reproduce selections from this book, write to Permissions,
Houghton Mifflin Company, 215 Park Avenue South,
New York, New York 10003.

www.houghtonmifflinbooks.com

This book is a work of fiction. Names, places, and incidents are
products of the author's imagination.
Any resemblance to actual events, persons, monkeys, elves, trolls,
and other creatures, great or small, pleasant or unpleasant,
is entirely coincidental.

The text of this book
is set in Mrs. Eaves and Benton Sans.
The illustrations are acrylic.
Monkeyworks mark rendered
in scratchboard by Elizabeth Traynor.

Library of Congress Cataloging-in-Publication Data

Kaczman, James.
Lucky monkey, unlucky monkey : a story / written and illustrated
by James Kaczman.
p. cm.

Summary: While Ed the monkey has the most wonderful day
imaginable, Ted the monkey faces everything from bad weather to
being chased by wild animals and an angry troll.

ISBN 978-0-618-63153-7

[1. Monkeys—Fiction. 2. Luck—Fiction. 3. Animals—Fiction. 4.
Humorous stories.] I. Title.

PZ7.K11646Luc 2008
[E]—dc22

2007034302

Printed in Singapore
TWP 10 9 8 7 6 5 4 3 2 1

Prelude

The following story is one of those in which the characters are not human beings; they are animals. But they wear clothing as human beings do, and think and talk like human beings do. This makes the characters extremely charming and interesting, as well as remarkably cute.

In some stories, such as *The Tale of Peter Rabbit*, certain animals wear shirts or jackets but, for some inexplicable reason, no pants. This, of course, makes no sense at all, so the animals in this story are fully clothed.

Also, in some stories, the animals wear clothing like human beings do, think like human beings do, and talk like human beings do, but for some reason, they still live in animal homes, such as a tree trunk or a hole in the ground.

This, of course, doesn't quite make sense if one thinks about it. So the animal characters in this story live in houses just as human beings do. This story is about two thinking, speaking, fully clothed, house-dwelling monkeys.

Chapter One

A SPLENDID DAY / A NOT SO SPLENDID DAY

"WHAT a beautiful day!" Ed the monkey said as he walked out of his small, just-the-right-size-for-a-monkey house. He was greeted by a bright sunny day, with flowers blooming, butterflies fluttering about, and friendly little animals happily hopping around. "Hello, sun! Good day to you, trees! Good morning, fluttering butterflies! Good morning, buzzing bees!" he said.

Meanwhile ... "What an awful day!" Ted the monkey said as he walked out of his small, just-the-right-size-for-a-monkey house. He was met by a forbidding sky of dark clouds, with large insects swarming about and frightening vermin crawling around. "Oh no—dark clouds! Oh no—creepy bugs! Oh dear—big rats! Eeeww—slimy slugs!" he said.

Stories for children often contain poetry, and the characters may speak in rhymes. People don't actually talk this way, though, because it is difficult for people to make everything they say rhyme all the time. Ed the monkey and Ted the monkey both speak in rhyme as they are introduced here as characters. But they don't speak in rhyme all the way through the story. This is because it is even more difficult for monkeys to make everything they say rhyme all the time.

Chapter Two

A PLEASANT WALK / AN UNPLEASANT WALK

"SINCE it is such a splendid bright sunny day, I think I will go for a walk," Ed the monkey said. He strolled along, looking rather handsome in his small, finely tailored, monkey-size suit.

Meanwhile ... Ted the monkey set out for a walk. "Since it looks like a storm is approaching, I think I will bring my umbrella," he said. He walked along, looking rather dashing in his small, stylish monkey-size suit. Ted believed in being prepared and always brought his umbrella with him when it looked like it might rain.

As Ed walked along he came upon a dog he had not met before. Ed shouted to the dog, "Hello there, doggie. How are you today? What's that you have in your paw? Do you want to play?"

Meanwhile ... as Ted walked along he also came upon a strange dog. Ted called out to the dog, "Hello there, doggie. How are you today? Why are you looking at me like that? Don't you want to play?"

Ed watched as the dog wagged his tail and bounded over to play. It was a friendly, playful dog.

"Yes! Good dog! Nice catch!" Ed happily shouted as they played.

It is not a good idea to play with a strange dog, even if it looks friendly and wags its tail. Most dogs are friendly and will not bite, but if you do not know the dog, it is wise to be very careful.

The other dog was not so friendly. "No! Bad dog! Please go away!" Ted desperately cried, dropping his umbrella as he fled.

It is not a good idea to play with a strange dog, even if it looks friendly and wags its tail. But it is an extremely bad idea to play with a strange dog that is growling and snarling so that its large, sharp white teeth show.

Chapter Three

SOME MORE NICE ANIMALS /
SOME MORE NOT SO NICE ANIMALS

AFTER playing with the friendly dog, Ed continued on his stroll. He came upon several woodland creatures as he walked along. First he came upon a friendly mouse. Then he met a pleasant chipmunk. After that he met a happy rabbit, a personable squirrel, a cheerful turtle, and a charming beaver. These new friends all joined Ed on his walk.

In the wild, most species, or different kinds of animals, usually don't spend much time being friendly with other species of animals. In real life, animals generally tend to stay among their own species. And so one would probably not see, for instance, a monkey being friends with a squirrel. But in children's stories, animals frequently have friendships with other species.

Figure A.
Two monkeys:
same species

Figure B.
Monkey and squirrel:
different species

Meanwhile ... as Ted ran from the angry dog, he also came upon several woodland creatures. But these animals were larger and not so pleasant. He came upon a horrible snake, who hissed and began chasing after him also.

Then a terrible bear joined in the pursuit. And after that a ferocious tiger, an awful crocodile, and a frightening gorilla all began angrily chasing after Ted.

Chapter Four

A LUCKY FIND / AN UNLUCKY FIND

As Ed walked along with his pleasant, charming new friends, he came upon a small chest. His friends watched as he picked up the chest and opened it. They were astonished to discover that the chest was filled with magic treasure!

A woodland elf, who is a magical wee person who lives in the woods, leaped out from behind a tree and said, "Hooray for you! You have found the magic treasure! You can spend it all at once! Or you can spend it at your leisure!"

Ed and his newfound friends jumped up and down and cheered this surprising and wonderful event.

Meanwhile ... Ted continued to flee from the group of mean, angry animals. Exhausted, he stopped for a moment and hid behind a tree to catch his breath. He looked down and saw a small chest. He picked up the chest and opened it. He was surprised to find that the chest was filled with magic treasure!

A woodland troll, who is an ugly, unpleasant creature somewhat larger than a woodland elf, leaped out from behind a tree and growled, "Why, I've caught you red-handed, trying to steal my treasure! I'll punish you for that, and then I'll eat you for good measure!"

The woodland troll swung a large wooden club above his head. Ted, who was horrified by this unusual and frightening event, dropped the treasure chest and ran.

Chapter Five

EVEN BETTER / EVEN WORSE

THE woodland elf led Ed and his friends to an enchanted woodland elf village of many little houses made from mushrooms nestled beneath the trees.

In children's stories, elves often live in mushrooms. This does not quite make sense if one thinks about it. A mushroom would actually be a rather unpleasant place to live, because mushrooms are damp and mushy inside. It also would smell funny. But because elves are magical creatures, nothing they do has to make any sense.

Meanwhile ... the horrible woodland troll, angrily swinging his large wooden club, chased after Ted. The angry animals all joined the troll in the chase.

Ted ran as fast as he could, but he could not escape from the horrible troll and the angry animals. He ran through dark forests and barren fields, tearing his clothing on branches and thorns along the way.

All the elves in the village gathered around Ed. Because he had found the magic treasure, they cheered and presented him with a crown and a scepter, making him honorary king of the woodland elves.

Then Ed, his friends, and all the elves sat down to a feast of delicious woodland elf food and drink. After the celebration had gone on for hours, Ed noticed it was getting late and decided it was time to return home. He thanked all his friends for the splendid afternoon and said goodbye.

Exhausted and desperate, Ted jumped into a stagnant, smelly swamp, dove beneath the mucky water, and hid among the tall reeds. The woodland troll and the angry animals could not see Ted where he was hiding, and they did not want to jump into the stinky swamp themselves.

So after a while they all wandered off, grumbling. Ted dragged himself out of the swamp and began to walk home, but then he realized that he was hopelessly lost.

Ideas about what certain types of animals are like are often based on old, untrue beliefs or fears and not facts. These ideas are called stereotypes. Small, cute animals are almost always portrayed as being nice, while large, non-vegetarian animals are usually depicted as being mean. For instance, snakes are often the villain in children's stories, when, in fact, snakes are fascinating creatures and some of them are kind, generous, witty, and charming, as well as being quite beautiful.

Chapter Six

A STRANGE ENCOUNTER / A STRANGER ENCOUNTER

As Ed strolled home, exhilarated by his experience, he came upon another monkey. "Look at that strange monkey," he thought. "He is certainly a dirty, smelly creature! And look at his shabby, filthy clothes! How horrid! How awful!"

As Ted trudged along, exhausted from his ordeal, he also came upon another monkey. "Look at that stranger," he thought. "He is certainly an impressive figure! And look at his splendid, finely tailored clothes! How handsome! How magnificent!"

"Can you help me?" Ted asked the well-dressed monkey. "I am lost. Can you tell me how to get back to town?"

Ed was a kind monkey, but he didn't know this strange monkey and he didn't like the way he looked or smelled. His first thought was to tell the other monkey to stay away from him. But he felt sorry for the unfortunate monkey.

"I would be happy to help you," the well-dressed monkey told Ted. "The town is that way. Good luck."

"Thank you," said Ted.

"You're welcome," answered the other monkey.

Ed, humming a cheerful tune, walked happily back to his house. The sun began to set, making the sky a beautiful pink color.

Ted, mumbling to himself, trudged slowly back to his house. The sky darkened and it began to rain.

Epilogue

THE next day ... "What an awful day!" Ed the monkey said as he walked out of his small, just-the-right-size-for-a-monkey house. "Not at all like yesterday, unfortunately!"

Meanwhile ... "What a beautiful day!" Ted the monkey said as he walked out of his small, just-the-right-size-for-a-monkey house. "Not at all like yesterday, thank goodness!"

The End

MONKEYS WITH HUMAN CHARACTERISTICS

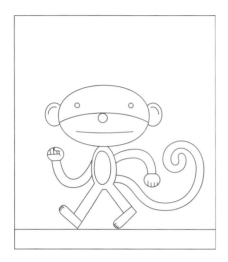

Figure A.
Thinking, speaking monkey
(Cute)

Figure B.
Thinking, speaking, fully clothed monkey
(Remarkably cute)

Figure C.
Thinking, speaking,
fully clothed, tree-dwelling monkey
(Does not quite make sense)

Figure D.
Thinking, speaking,
fully clothed, house-dwelling monkey
(Makes sense)